The Nexus Adventures:
Lunar Leap

By Valerie Emuakhagbon
Illustrated by Johannes Christian

In their cozy room, where stuffed animals covered most surfaces and colorful posters decorated the walls, Lily and Max always had fun . They were the dynamic duo of imagination and discovery. These 8-year-old twins were best friends. And they were constantly ready to explore the wonders of the world together.

Their room was the best place for adventures. At any given time, they had rocket ships made of cardboard, castles surrounded by toy armies, and treasure maps stretched across the floor.

On this evening , Lily and Max were focused on space. Lily, with her love of learning, held a toy telescope. Max , with his vast energy and brave heart, held a book with pictures of planets and stars.

As they played, their voices filled the room with laughter and excitement. Lily gazed out the window. "Look, Max! I can see the stars! They're like tiny diamonds in the sky."

Max continued flipping through his book. "Did you know, Lily, the sun is a giant star? It's so hot that it makes our days bright and warm!"

"Max, wouldn't it be amazing to visit outer space?" Lily said with a grin. "I wish we could see the stars up close. I bet we'd find incredible things up there."

"That would be so cool!" Max said . He rummaged through their closet, looking for a book about the moon. At that moment, a shiny, red button, hidden on the wall behind their clothes, caught his eye.

"Lily, look what I found!" exclaimed Max. "I've never seen this button in here before. I wonder what it does."

Lily joined him in the closet, looking at the knob. "Only one way to find out," Max said. He jammed his fist square on the button.

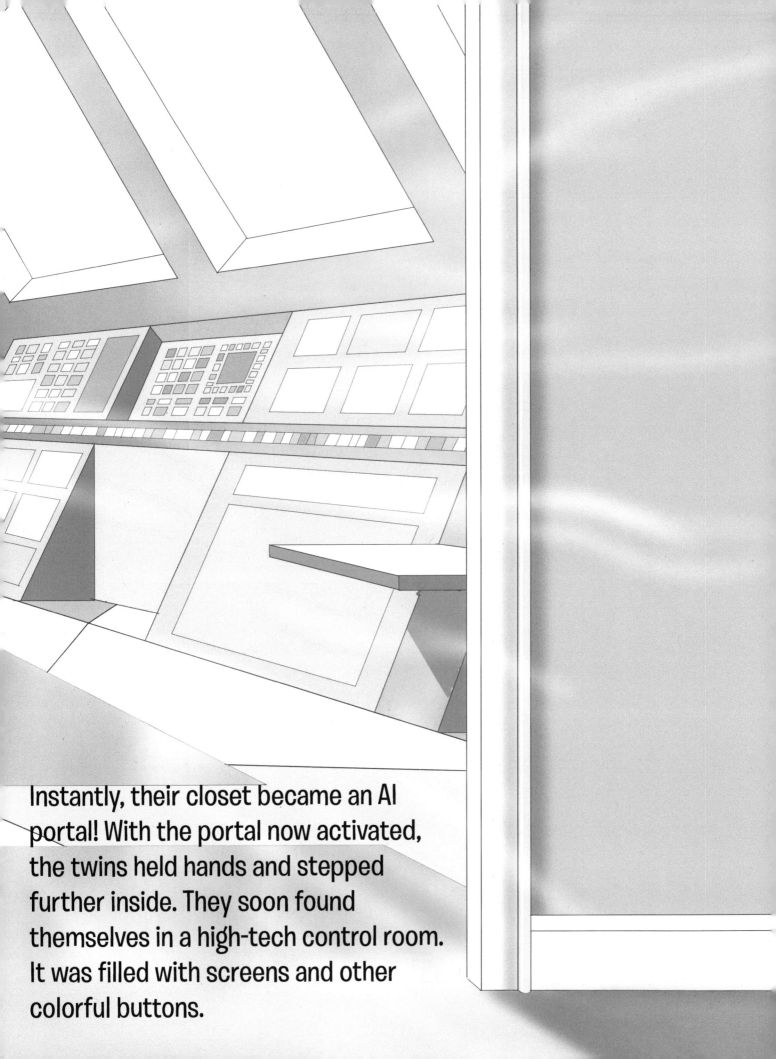

Instantly, their closet became an AI portal! With the portal now activated, the twins held hands and stepped further inside. They soon found themselves in a high-tech control room. It was filled with screens and other colorful buttons.

At first, their mouths just hung open. "What is this place?" Lily finally asked.

"This is Nexus," a voice said from behind them. The twins quickly turned around to see a smiling, friendly robot. "And I am Luna, the AI assistant!" she said, shaking their hands. "Nexus is a portal that can take you anywhere in the universe."

After they introduced themselves, Luna showed the twins around the Nexus control room. She taught them all about the buttons, knobs, and wheels.

With bright eyes
and a big smile,
Max asked, "Could we
go to the moon?"

"Of course!" Luna replied.

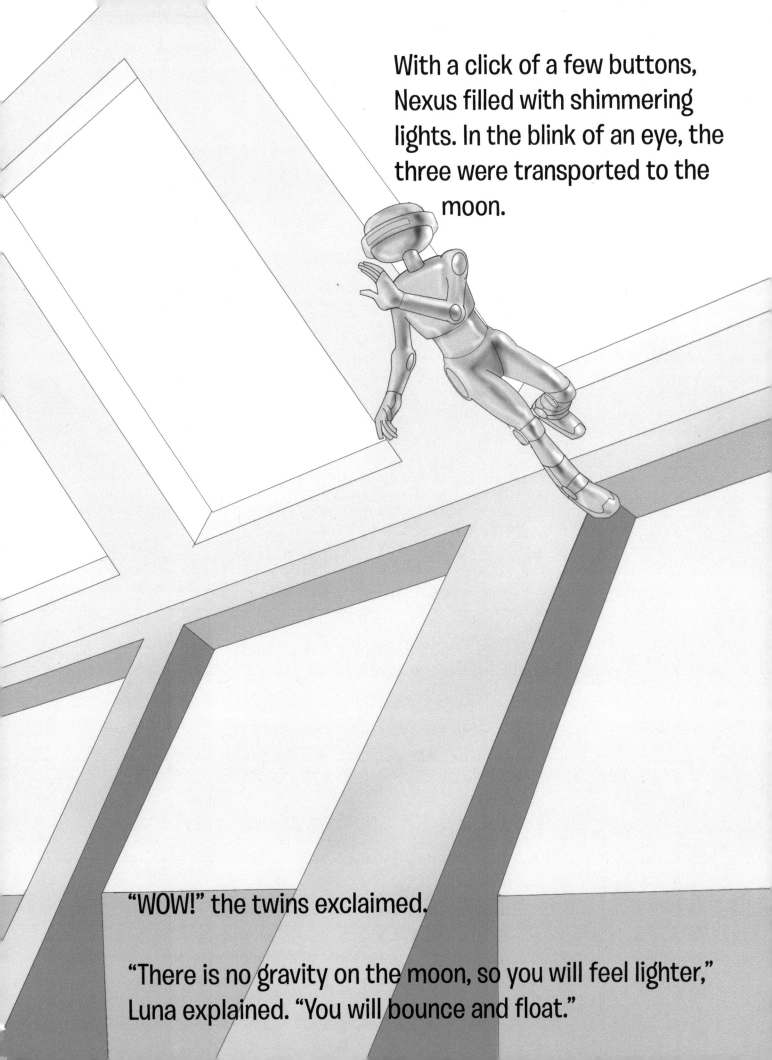

With a click of a few buttons, Nexus filled with shimmering lights. In the blink of an eye, the three were transported to the moon.

"WOW!" the twins exclaimed.

"There is no gravity on the moon, so you will feel lighter," Luna explained. "You will bounce and float."

When they arrived and bobbed along the surface, Luna shared interesting facts about the moon. Max and Lily collected moon rocks for their pockets. "We're like real astronauts," Max exclaimed.

The adventure continued when they approached a group of colorful, fluffy moon creatures. "Hello, we come in peace," said Lily. The beings responded with friendly hand gestures.

"Help! I don't know how to get down!" Max called. Lily looked at Luna, panic rising.

But Luna remained calm. "We need to think like scientists. Remember, the moon's gravity is much weaker than Earth's."

Lily had an idea. "What if we use our space ropes?
We could throw one end to Max and pull him back!"

"Good idea!" Luna said.

Lily secured herself and Luna by tying their end of the rope
around a large rock. Then, she tossed the other end toward Max.
"Got it!" he shouted.

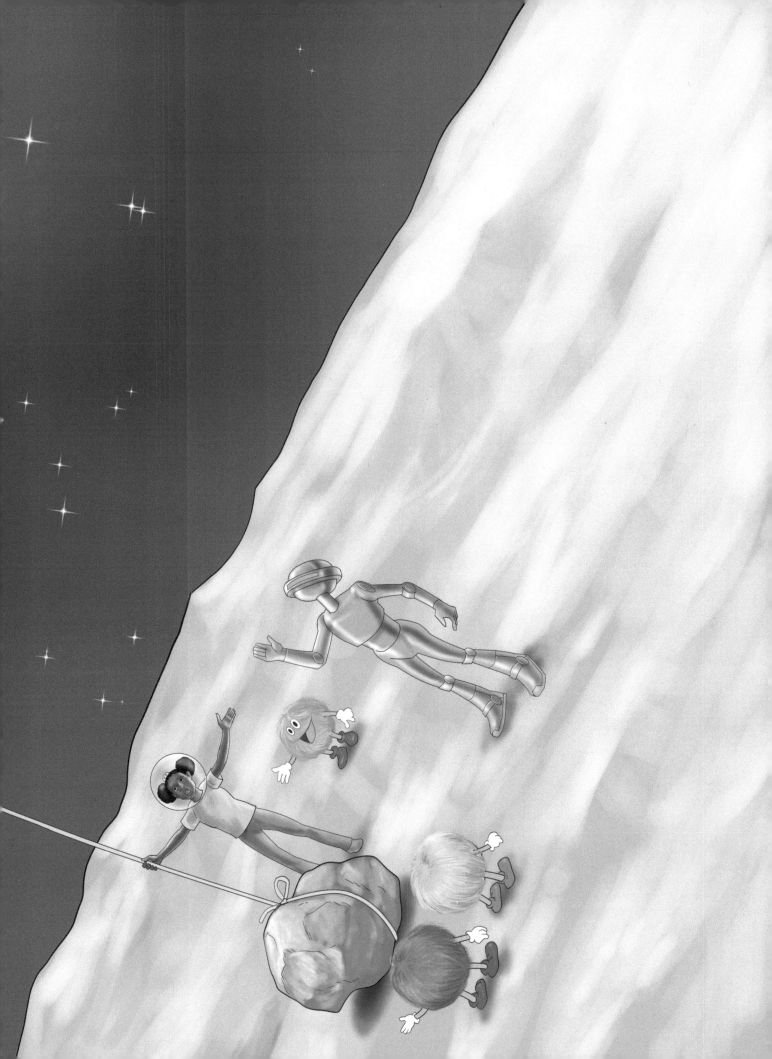

Lily, Luna, and the creatures slowly pulled Max back toward the moon's surface. With them all working together, Max's feet finally touched the ground again.

He was happy and hugged Lily tightly. "Thank you! I thought I'd be stuck floating forever!"

Lily laughed. "It's all about teamwork and thinking creatively."

After tiring themselves out from play, everyone in the group enjoyed a picnic. They ate moon cheese and drank bubbly cosmic juice.

"This is the best adventure ever!" Lily announced.

When the sun set without warning, Max and Lily realized the time had come to head home. They hugged and thanked their new moon friends with a promise to visit again. Luna then transported them back to Earth.

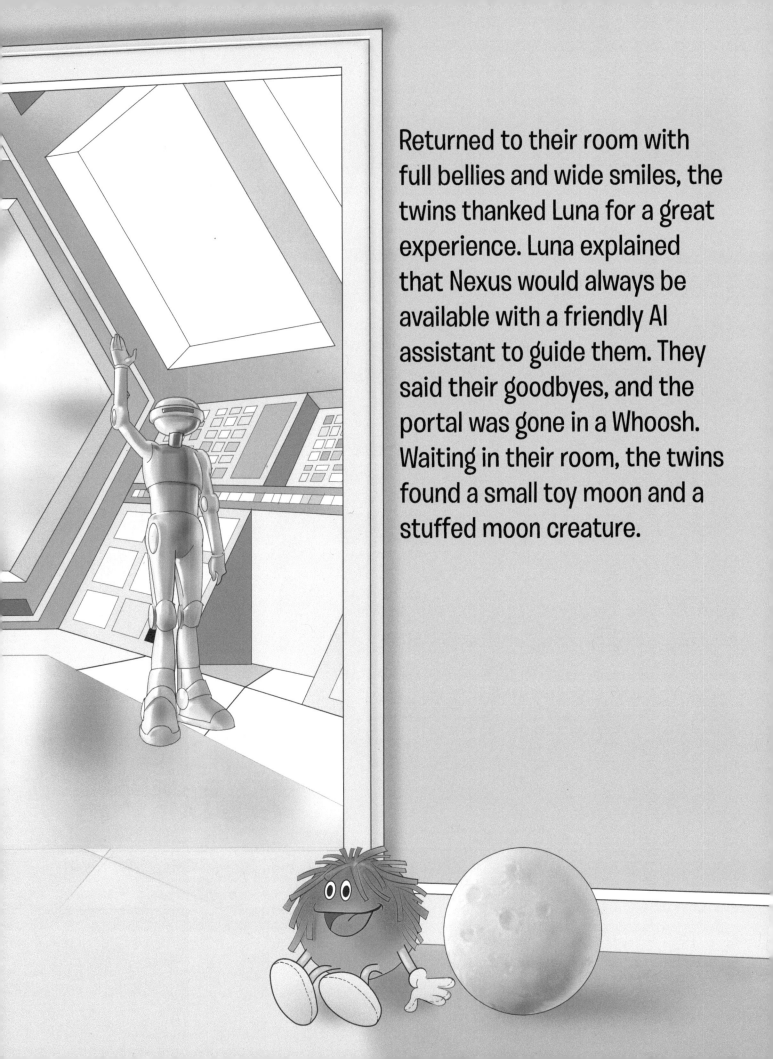

Returned to their room with full bellies and wide smiles, the twins thanked Luna for a great experience. Luna explained that Nexus would always be available with a friendly AI assistant to guide them. They said their goodbyes, and the portal was gone in a Whoosh. Waiting in their room, the twins found a small toy moon and a stuffed moon creature.

Yawning, Lily and Max then got ready for bed. They brushed their teeth and said their prayers. Into the dark room, Lily whispered, "Where will we go next time?"

Max was also snuggled in his bed. "Our future adventures could take us anywhere," he said. "With Nexus and Luna, this was just the beginning!"

All glory to God.

To my loving family:
Thank you for all of your
encouragement and inspiration.

A special thank you to C.I.
Thank you for planting the
seed that led to this story.

Milton Keynes UK
Ingram Content Group UK Ltd.
UKHW052139190724
445932UK00003B/19